KEATON FINDS EDEN

DANNY O'KELLY

authorHOUSE®

AuthorHouse™
1663 Liberty Drive
Bloomington, IN 47403
www.authorhouse.com
Phone: 833-262-8899

Published by AuthorHouse 01/17/2023

ISBN: 978-1-7283-7778-0 (sc)
ISBN: 978-1-7283-7779-7 (e)

Library of Congress Control Number: 2023900982

Print information available on the last page.

Any people depicted in stock imagery provided by Getty Images are models,
and such images are being used for illustrative purposes only.
Certain stock imagery © Getty Images.

This book is printed on acid-free paper.

Because of the dynamic nature of the Internet, any web addresses or
links contained in this book may have changed since publication and
may no longer be valid. The views expressed in this work are solely those
of the author and do not necessarily reflect the views of the publisher,
and the publisher hereby disclaims any responsibility for them.

Hello, my name is Keaton, I was born near Fort Bliss, TX, about ten minutes from El Paso and the Rio Grande river. I was just a young boy with dreams and high ambitions. My dad had always talked about me becoming a cowboy. It was his dream, not mine. My father's name was Jack and my mother's name was Jill. Yes, and I've heard the story 1000 times about them going up a hill to get a bucket of water. My father was not the Jack that climbed up the beanstalk looking for a goose that laid a golden egg. My dad's ambitions were a lot greater than finding a goose that laid a golden egg. Although this goose may have solved a lot of his problems, he was more interested in solving the world's problems. This was my father Jack and he did have a last name, but I'll tell you about it later.

Dad lived most of his life just outside of El Paso, Texas. When he was very young, he was also very ambitious. He was always dreaming and reaching for the stars. He felt there was nothing too hard to achieve if you wanted it bad enough, although his family was considered very poor. They were only poor in financial assets. Hopes and dreams didn't cost anything and wishing for a better tomorrow was not a liability. It was a goal that Jack intended to achieve.

My dad started driving at 10 or 12 years old, but to hear him tell it, he's always been driving even before he learned to walk. Jack was quiet and an aggressive person. He didn't want to wait around or anything very much. I suppose that is why he married my mom Jill when she was only 15 years old. Dad had a lot of sayings. One of his favorites was, "Do as I say, not as I have done." He was also quite an outdoorsman. Instead of going to school and learning to read and write, dad would spend his school days playing hooky. If you don't know what hooky is, dad said that's good. Dad said it caused him a whole lot of grief and time that he wished he had spent in the classroom. Another one of his sayings is, "No need crying over spilt milk. Clean up the mess and keep moving." Even though dad knew that what he had done in skipping school was wrong. Skipping school was a loss in his educational learning. Dad used to say in front of older people that, "book learning is very good and needed, but what the younger generation needs as much as book learning is some down home common sense." He used to say, "Common sense will take you a long way down the right path on life's journey and you will know the tree by the fruit that it bears, the leaves it sheds and by feeling its bark." He said, "All fish are not the same, some have scales while others have skins, some snakes are dangerous and even have poisonous venom and other snakes are harmless and actually help all mankind." Then dad would say, "but for the life of me I can't understand why God made mosquitos." The first few years dad's and mom's marriage was a struggle. Not in their love for one another, but trying to survive in this dog eat dog world. They both talked one night before they went to sleep. Dad said, "Jill, I've got to make a decision and I have to make it tomorrow." That next day, dad jumped right out of the frying pan into the fire. Dad joined the military. That evening, when he got back home from the recruiting station, he told my mom what he had done. Although she did not understand it, she knew her husband Jack. He said, "you will have to move back home with your mom and dad for a while." Her mom and dad had no other children. She was an only child and he knew that they would be glad to get their daughter back home for a while. Uncle Sam was glad to get a new recruit. There goes the story of my dad and mom, Jack and Jill. I was born while dad was in the military. I went to school while dad was still in active duty service. I guess that makes me a full fledged military brat. As I told you earlier, my name is Keaton. This book is about me and my father Jack, and how we saved the world, and I found Eden.

I can remember as a young boy growing up in South Texas going fishing and hunting with my dad or maybe going with him and mom on our summer vacation to Galveston to the beach. I can even remember during these times of my life dad would say, "this world is getting into a bad mess." He said they were digging a hole so deep that they will never climb back out of it, but he would always say with every problem, there is a remedy and for everything there is a solution. If people would just slow down long enough to smell the roses. Most of the problems in this world are simply man-made. He said, "the bible stated they will tear down barns just to build bigger ones. A family of three or four will have a five or six bedroom house and they never have anyone over to stay all night. Trees are being cut down to build these houses and shopping centers. The rainforest is being destroyed. When it rains, the water has no way of seeping into the ground because of so much concrete and asphalt being poured." I know my mother must have got tired of listening to him carry on for hours. I know I did. He used to tell me the right way to fish. The right way to shoot a gun and the right way to play baseball. You might think that my dad was some kind of know it all. Well, I didn't take him that way because he always seemed to have a way of making it interesting. He might seem to be going in a roundabout way to get his point across, but when he did, it seemed to have a way of sticking. While dad was in the military, he never seemed to bring his military circumstances home to the family. Dad was not a dedicated Christian man. I know he believed in God because he talked about him all the time. He believed there was a place called Heaven for those that believed in God and a place called Hell for those who rejected him or his son Jesus. He told me that one day, God will destroy this earth, but not the way it is being destroyed now. Dad did not know anything about what they now call the New Green Deal. Yes, there was some talk about climate change and global warming, but that kind of talk had been going on for decades. Dad would say, "On one side of the coin, they are right, but on the other side they have missed it like shooting at the broadside of a barn." I can remember going to some isolated places when I was very young with dad and he would say, "I don't think anyone else has ever been here before, Do you Keaton?" Kind of like Adam the first man that God created there in Eden. Adam's footprint was the

only human footprints in Eden at least before Eve came along. He would look back at our footprints and say, "I bet you that we are the only people that have ever walked down this path before." Then, he would take a big snort of fresh air and say, "No I don't smell anyone, do you?" then laugh with a chuckle. I remember when I was eight, maybe nine year old, dad told me I'd have to be the man of the house. He was going on a field exercise in the military. They would take him away from home for 2–3 weeks. Mom and I were quite used to that being a military family, so we just battened down the hatches and waited for him to return. However, when dad returned, he was different, something had changed or should I say something had changed him. There had been a very violent storm the first two or three days dad was gone. Mom and I thought very little of it and carried on with our everyday lives. Dad had been found lying in an ACP tent unconscious. No one knew what had happened to him. They took him to the military hospital to be checked out. They found nothing wrong with him, but they continued to monitor him. For the first few days, his speech seemed to be slurred. Some of his motor skills also seemed to be affected. No one had noticed, but the color of his eyes had changed. The paramedics and the doctors wrote it off as maybe a slight stroke, or maybe a lightning strike had hit the ACP tent he was staying in. As I mentioned before, there had been a thunderstorm that night. After a few days, they released him from the hospital and sent him back to his unit. Mom was never notified that this event had even happened. A few years later, the pieces came together.

When dad came home from a field exercise, his demeanor had changed. I'm not saying that he was mean, aggressive, or confrontational. He was just different. He was more serious minded about things. I can't say that he never joked or wanted to cut up. He did all that but in a different kind of way. All the things he used to talk about like hunting, fishing, or gardening, he never talked about anymore. His attention seemed to be towards the cosmos, the heavens. My dad talked about the stars and constellations, but his number one thing to talk about was the moon. He seemed to be mesmerized by Neil Armstrong walking on the moon. He must have replayed and watched him walking on the moon saying, "one small step for man, one giant step for mankind" more than 1000 times. In the latter days of his life, he would say they had the right idea, but they missed the point.

One day about six months after he had returned from his military field exercise event, I noticed another change in dad's face. He never blinked his eyes. I don't think he even closed his eyes to sleep. I did not say anything to mom because she seemed to be worried enough, so I kept it all to myself. No one could help but notice when he began to build his contraction. He was kind of like the man in the science fiction thriller "Close Encounters" of the third kind. I saw him take a piece from a car engine, then another piece from an outside air conditioning unit. He had all kinds of pieces of electronic equipment that he had gathered. Then, he began to put it all together. When he got it all together, it was no larger than a shoe box. It had an on and off switch and a gauge like a car fuel gauge that ranged from zero to ten. After about a month of working on his contraction,

I heard him say, "I think I've got it." Then he looked at me and said, "Keaton, you want to go with me on Saturday?" He was always excited to go with his dad, but he said, "we are going" with a twinkle in his eyes, "hopefully to a place where no one has gone before." Dad had always been a fan of the TV show Star Trek, so I immediately knew what he was talking about. I just did not know why. When Saturday finally rolled around, we started on our trip. I said, "Dad, where are we going?" He said, "Son, you remember we used to go to those isolated places and I jokingly told you that no one had ever been there before? Well, I want to find out just how true or untrue that statement is. That is why I brought the Numerator with us." I said, "You mean that contraction that you built?" "Yes, I call it the Numerator." My dad said. I replied, "Why do you call it that?" My dad said, "Well, I had to call it something and that is the best name I could come up with." I asked my dad, "What does a Numerator do?" He said, "A Numerator counts as a part of a whole. You will learn that later on in school." Dad and I finally got to the isolated place and dad turned his device on. Then he looked at me and shook his head and said, "Just as I thought. The Numerator confirms what I believed that we have destroyed our firmaments." "What did you say dad, firmaments? What do you mean firmaments?" "I will try to show you the best I know how. The numerator that I created confirmed to me the idea that we are destroying ourself and making our planet unlivable. High above our planet about ten to fifteen miles is an area known as our stratosphere. There is a ring known to scientists as the ozone layer and it shields all living things from the sun's harmful ultraviolet radiation, therefore it protects us.

There are large holes being formed in the ozone layer letting the harmful ultraviolet radiation penetrate to Earth. This ozone layer must be repaired. Pointing fingers at what caused it, is not repairing it. It is like having a glass sitting on a shelf and figuring out who knocked it off and broke it. The fact of the matter is that the glass is broken and it must be fixed. Some would say that it is impossible, but it is. Someone made the glass before it was broken, so it can be repaired because all things are possible if you're willing to do it. Glass can be put back together and the ozone layer can be repaired." I was only about nine years old when dad took me to that area that we called the isolated place. Dad said we are not the first nor the only people to ever walk there. When he turned his numerator on, it registered .3 Quadro Felix. When I asked him what Quadro Felix meant, he said, ".3 thousand people have been there in the last five or six years." That is very small considering the population of the Earth. Dad then got a five gallon bucket of sand from the isolated place and took it in with us. He said, "I've got one more experiment I need to do to confirm my theory and show that my Numerator is right." We proceeded to a park just outside of El Paso. It was nighttime and dad took his Numerator and turned it on. He proceeded to check the Quadro Felix number at the city park. After checking his device, he looked at me and said, "I was right, my Numerator has confirmed what I believed to be true. The firmaments have been destroyed and there are zero Quadro Felix. Now I need to know if they can be repaired or should I say replaced." Dad, not being a very religious man, prayed a prayer that night. I recall as a young boy what I heard him say. He prayed, "Lord God, you are the creator of all things.

Mankind has let you down from the beginning therefore Adam was dispersed from the garden of Eden. This planet that you have given us, we have abused, but as long as we are in these mortal bodies, we have no other place to call home. God this sand that I have brought in from the isolated place is not your original firmaments, but God let it be an example representing the firmaments as olive oil is to the Holy Spirit." Dad took the sand in the five gallon bucket and began to throw it up into the sky as a child would be playing in the sand pile. As the sand began to flow down from the sky, the sky began to crystalize in a blue, greenish tint. I had never seen anything like it before. After he did this procedure, he took his Numerator and turned it back on, but this time the reading showed Quadro Felix .01. It was only a trace, but enough to show Jack, my dad, that the ozone layer could be repaired.

When we returned home the next day, I thought that Jack would be rejoiceful, but that was not the case. He was like a man standing in the river knowing what was on the other side, but unable to get there. From time to time, I would see him get his device out, also known as the Numerator, and modify it or look at it. He was getting close to his military career coming to an end and I showed very little interest in following his footsteps. He did not know what he would do when his military career came to an end. It had been about five years since dad's experience with the field exercise. It wasn't talked about nor was it forgotten. I felt someday it would all come back full throttle. Sometimes, I would see dad writing in books and sometimes the book was the Bible. Out in the shop, dad would sometimes say, "Keaton, don't forget to look in here." I was almost 13 years old, about to start Junior High. School seemed to be a drag, I never took it to be very important. I guess I was a chip off the old block, but I never played hooky like someone else that I know. The only thing that I really liked about school was football. I played what dad said was the most important position on the team, free safety. He used to tell me I was the last line of defense. We always had our games on Thursday. The high school always had Friday night because they were seniors. Jack used to say, "You will get your chance to play some Friday night and the whole world will be watching." I never questioned him. Why he said "the whole world" I do not know. It was only a high school football game. One Thursday night after a football game, we were all going out to get a pizza or a taco to celebrate. It was my birthday and I would be 13. That evening before the game, dad told my mom Jill that he did not feel like going to the game, but that he would meet us at the restaurant for the birthday celebration after the game was over. After winning the game, I was jubilating and could not wait to tell my dad that I scored on a pick six from my free safety position on the last play of the game. However, dad was not at the restaurant. Mom and I knew that there was something wrong or he would have been there. We tried to eat our cake, be sociable, and leave as soon as possible. When we arrived home, dad was sitting in his favorite chair holding a picture of us on his lap, that was on top of the Numerator that he built. When the paramedics came and took him to the hospital, the doctor said that he didn't believe he had a heart attack, but his heart just stopped beating.

My dad Jack died on my 13th birthday. I remember when I came home that night and saw him sitting in the chair. His eyes

were wide open. One eye was blue and the other eye was green. Five years ago before the accident, both of dad's eyes were brown. After the funeral, mom and I began to confront one another about dad and the changes that we had both noticed. We had never discussed it with each other about dad's eyes changing color. She said she did not want to upset me and I told her that is the same way I felt about her. We also discussed that his eyes never blinked. Mom told me that dad slept with his eyes open. We both agreed that something estranged had happened to dad on the field exercise and he never got over it. Dad had a military funeral with a military honor guard which presented mom with a folded flag. Dad's commanding officer was there and sometime during the funeral, mom asked him to droop by our house because she had some questions that she would like him to answer. After several days, Captain Shea came to our house. He was very apologetic for the accident and stated that if there is anything he could do to please let him know. After a very cordial visitation, mom said, "Captain Shea, there is something I would like to ask you. I know you were not Jack's commanding officer, but maybe you can still find out if something might have happened." Mom then proceeded to tell Captain Shea about the field exercise and dad returning and his eyes being a different color. Captain Shea seemed very curious about what mom had told him. He told us he would check it out the best he could and get back with us as soon as possible. Mom thanked him for coming by. Then, Captain Shea looked at me and said, "Is this Jack's boy?" Mom said, "Yes it is, that is Keaton. Jack died on his 13th birthday." He replied, "I know that must be hard son, but I want you to know God is a good God and everything that he does is for a reason. He has something in store for you, Keaton.

Slowly the days passed by after dad's funeral. Mom and everyone else said that we will have to pick up the pieces and move on because that is what Jack would have wanted. I suppose that the first year was the hardest for me and Mom. We were trying to get used to doing things on our own. My job was simply to go to school and get an education because that is what Dad would have wanted. Mom mostly took care of the housework, but she did get a part-time job from time to time. Dad provided for the family and all of our financial needs. Just in case something happened to him, mom and I would not have to worry. About two years after Dad's passing, I was in the garage cleaning up when I remembered Jack telling me not to forget to look in here. I didn't know what he meant, but when I looked in the cubby hole I couldn't believe what I was seeing. Dad had placed two paid up life insurance policies. These were beside what mom had gotten out of their security box. There was another letter addressed to my mom saying it was important on the outside of the letter. When I took the items to mom, her face went blank as if she didn't know what to say, but neither did I. Although mom and I did not discuss it at this time, we both knew that dad was leaving behind something much more important than money. When mom sat down to open the letter that had very important written on the outside, I couldn't help but wonder what was so important. When my mom opened the letter, her eyes began to bulge out as if she couldn't believe what she was reading. With a semi chuckle in her voice she said, "It is about the Numerator that he made. He said that someday you and the Numerator would save the world. He is also talking about you becoming an astronaut, but said that you must not join NASA because in a few years there will be another space program and that he would like for you to join. He also states that Captain Shea will help you get started in this program when he comes to visit the second time." At this point I stopped mom from reading. I said, "Mom, how did he know that Captain Shea had already come and what do you suppose he meant by saying another space program? And for me to be an astronaut? I haven't finished high school." "I don't know son, but I know your dad was not a nut." Mom said. There has to be something behind all of this and we have to figure it out. We both agreed not to tell anyone about the letter. Many people thought dad was weird anyways and that he was probably delirious when he wrote it.

One day mom said there was a knock on the door. I was in school, but mom was at home alone. Mom went to the door and thought it was Captain Shea. However, it was not Captain Shea. It was Col Shea. Mom, knowing who it was, let him in with a smile on her face and said, "Congratulations, Col. Shea, Jack would be so proud of you. What brings you this way?" He said, "Keaton, remember the last time I was here, you asked me a question about Jack's eyes changing color?" Shea looked at me and said, "You know the hands of justice sometimes move very slowly, but I never stopped trying to find out about your mystery. Although the mystery is hidden deep in conspiracy and top secret, I will try to tell you about that night and what I think happened to Jack the best I can." There was an experiment that night by NASA that most of the soldiers, including Jack knew nothing about. NASA had exploded a satellite in orbit. No one or anything seemed to be affected by this explosion. There was a violent storm that night and no one thought anything about the thunder or rain. They found Jack unconscious and took him to the hospital. After some normal and should I say abnormal test, it was determined by the federal government that Jack would be all right. He would be sent back to the unit and everyone would keep their mouth shut. No one suspected there was anything wrong with Jack and no one noticed his eyes had changed color. What I have told you is a deep secret and I must have your word that what has been said in this house will not leave this house. Then mom said, "Col Shea, Jack had other issues and that could have been the reason that he died." Shea said, "Ma'am, I am sorry, but I do not have the answer for that. Because of this tragedy and grief of losing your loved one, I have been sent by the President of the United States to offer you a settlement. Although the U.S. government does not take blame for the tragedy, we will try to compensate you to the best of our ability. If there is anything we can do to help you, please tell me now." For a few moments, Jill pondered his offer in her mind. She knew that they were financially sound because Jack had already seen to that. Then, she remembered Jack's letter where he stated that it was very important and that Shea would be coming a second time. She looked and turned to Shea and looked him in the eyes. She said, "Tell me about this new space program that is now being started." Col. Shea looked at her and said, "How would you know about the new space program? This information has not been spoken to the public by anyone. It is also top secret, so how do you know about it?" She looked at him and said, "Jack told me all about it." He replied, "There is a new space program starting up and in fact, they are drafting new astronaut recruits this fall. That is if they get it on the budget." Jill said, "Be assured, Jack told me it would be on budget. I ask from the president of the United States that my son Keaton be one of the first recruits for astronauts in the space force. Shea replied, "I don't know ma'am, can you give me a few days?" "Sure," said Jill.

In a couple of hours Keaton arrived home from school driving his ragtop Jeep. I may be a little biased in my opinion because I am his mom, but he is quite a nice looking young man. He kind of reminds me of his dad when he was that age. It was such a long time ago. I wanted to tell Keaton about our visitor that came by, but there were still a lot of unanswered questions. I am sure Keaton had a lot of questions also. I decided it wasn't the right time to mention it. Keaton had questions of his own like, "What's for dinner?" And then he surprised me. "Never mind I am going out for dinner tonight and I am taking Hannah with me," Keaton said. Jill said, "What are you doing tonight and who are you going with?" Keaton said, "I am going out for dinner with Hannah." "Okay Keaton, but who is Hannah?" Jill asked. "It is just a girl mom. She goes to my school, she is in my science class, and she is on the cheerleading squad. We agreed to go steady." Jill said, "Go steady? It's the first date you have been on." Keaton replied, "Well to be honest, it is the first date you have known about." "You have been keeping her a secret from me? Who is her mom and dad and where do they live?" Jill asked. "Okay mom, that's enough questions for right now. You might get to see her tonight after we have eaten dinner. If it is not too late, I will swing by here, but you have got to promise me no 3rd degree questioning. Is that a deal mom?" Keaton asked. "That is a deal, son. Is she a blonde or a brunette?" Jill asked. Keaton replied, "No mom, she is gray headed with what little hair she still has. She is 60 years old."

Jill was so excited and she could not wait to see her. She stared at every car that went by in the driveway thinking it may be them. Keaton had never shown much interest in girls. Jill thought it was just the trauma that his life had been through, but I was so glad that he found Hannah. Just like the girl in the Bible. Jill said, "Hannah is such a sweet name. I bet she is a good girl. She better be or this will be the last date if I have anything to do with it." It felt like an eternity until Keaton's Jeep pulled into the driveway. Jill was peeping through the window watching them as they got out of the Jeep. Keaton got out first and went to the passenger side and assisted a beautiful young lady out of his Jeep. At this time, Jill had to scramble from her peeping perch to an easy chair in the living room. When the door opened and the couple walked into the living room, Jill pretended to be reading a fashion magazine. She then sprang to her feet and said, "It is very nice to meet you" shaking Hannah's hand. Then Hannah said, "it is nice to meet you too, Mrs. Ripper." So, there you have it, Jack's last name. He is dead now, so it doesn't hurt telling his last name. Jack never did like his last name. Jack Ripper, the kids used to tease him and called him Jack the Ripper. He never did mind the beanstalk or the bucket on the hill, but he could not stand Jack the Ripper. I guess it was an honor thing.

Hannah was a beautiful girl. She was the same age as Keaton. They had known each other all through high school. Hannah had blonde sandy hair and dark skin. Her family was very highly thought of in the community, but Hannah seemed to be a down to earth girl who was well mannered. Later on, Jill told Keaton she thought he had done a good job choosing Hannah for his date. Keaton told his mom that he thought she would like a nice girl. That summer after high school graduation, Keaton and Hannah spent a lot of time together. She was either at Keaton's house or he was over there with her mom and dad. Life was going well and I suppose Jack would have been pleased with our progress. It had been six months since Col. Shea had been by the house and we talked about Jack. I hope he has not forgotten about us.

One Saturday morning, Keaton got up and was watching some college football on TV. Jill said, "Keaton, are you and Hannah not going out today?" Keaton replied, "Yes, we are later on." I could tell from his attitude that something was not right. I spoke up in a compassionate voice and said, "What's bothering you son?" Keaton said, "Hannah is moving away. I mean she isn't moving, but she is going away. She is starting school in the fall at SMU University. She wants to become a psychologist. I told her she should have met my dad, but I was joking. In fact, she wants me to register and join her this fall at the same university, but I don't know what I want to do. Some days I want to go and then the next day I change my mind. What do you think I would be good at?" Jill said, "You will be good at anything you set your mind to and there is nothing that you can't do if you want it bad enough." Keaton replied,

"That sounds like something dad would say. He used to say those same words all the time." Jill said, "I can remember him saying that too and I know that he would want you to be happy in any decision you make. I also know what he wanted you to be." Keaton said with an elevated voice, "Please mom, don't go there. Dad did not know what he was talking about. Especially when he wrote the letter that I found in the garage that said VERY IMPORTANT. You know that had to be the truth." Jill said, "I am sorry son, but I don't know that to be the truth because I had a visitor come and see me a few months back and we talked about your dad Jack." Keaton asked, "Who was it mom and why did you not tell me about it?" Jill answered and said, "Well Keaton, I was waiting to know a little more about the situation. The visitor was Col. Shea and he came a second time as Jack had written in his letter." Keaton said, "Well mom that was probably just a courtesy call which is why he came by." Jill explained, "Col Shea had tried to explain what happened the night that dad was on the field exercise." Keaton said, "You mean something really happened to dad that changed the color of his eyes?" As Keaton was talking, he was also turning the TV down and moving closer to the front seat. "Yes Shea said there was an explosion." Jill said. By this time, Keaton was standing on the floor and he had turned the TV off. Keaton said, "They knew it all along and they kept it from us. I am going to the military base." Jill said, "No, it is not like that at all. There was a satellite explosion, but nothing was damaged and no one was hurt is what they thought. Col. Shea said they did not know about his eyes changing color. While Shea was visiting, he gave his condolences and apologized on behalf of the United States government for our loss. He said to tell you hello and that he would be back to see us again soon." Keaton said, "I smell a rat and it is a dead rat that I am going to find where the stink is coming from. We will talk about this later. I am going to Hannah's house. Jill said, "Be careful and do not stay out too late." When Keaton left to go pick up Hannah, I knew I had not told him everything. His plate was full and he couldn't carry anymore. I didn't want to say anything about the promise of the president and what Col. Shea had told me, but I also knew that I could not drop the ball. I knew I had to get back in touch with Col. Shea and find out about the promise he had made me. I knew Jack wanted Keaton to become an astronaut. I saw pictures in some magazines where Jack had put Keaton's name next to some astronaut pictures. This was all a mystery and I didn't know how it would end, but I felt that Jack knew what he was talking about. I did not understand it and it did sound stupid to me that my husband had built a Numerator out of scrap, and said the ozone layer needed to be repaired by replacing the firmaments in space by our son "Keaton the Astronaut."

The next week was very hectic to say the least. With Hannah going off to college, Keaton seemed concerned about their future, but he blamed it on worrying about her safety. He also didn't know what direction in life he should be pursuing. As for me, one of my top priorities was to find and talk to Col. Shea. I wanted to go down to Fort Bliss and check with the personnel resource department about locating Col. Shea, but I had also scheduled for the carpet in the upstairs bedrooms to be cleaned. The heating and air conditioning tech was supposed to come out this week and service our unit. If that was not enough, the free will society was to come one day and clean out our garage of the usable merchandise that I had donated. This was a really hard pill to swallow because most of the items being donated were Jack's. Keaton had told me that he agreed the items needed to be disposed of or given to an organization. Keaton did not want any part in giving the items away. When he came home Monday evening, he said, "Mom on Thursday I will be going with Hannah to register for college. She told me she would like for me to tag along, so if there is nothing pressing for me to do, I would like to go with her. Would that be okay?" I said, "Sure Son, there is nothing much happening around here." (I am lying to him again.) I thought with him out of the house, Thursday may give me the opportunity to try to find Col. Shea. There was a lot going on with the heating and air tech supposed to be coming out and the free will society coming to clean out the garage. My husband Jack was not what you would consider a pack rat, but he would keep things that always seem important at a later time in life. In the present, the items seem more like junk or a piece of coal. However, in the future a piece of coal would later turn into a piece of gold. I was always skeptical about throwing things away that Jack wanted to keep. The night we found Jack's body deceased, he was holding a device that he had built and called the Numerator. This device seemed very important to Jack therefore, I could not discard it. The man from the free will society found a shoe box half full of note binders. The outside of the box was duct taped and Keaton's name written on the tape. There were a few other items that I could not seem to depart with.

Early Thursday morning, Keaton left to go with Hannah to register for college. I left for Fort Bliss, Texas. When I got there, I went straight to the post locator. I told the receptionist that I was trying to find Col. Shea and I proceeded to tell her that he had been my husband's commanding officer. I told her I needed to talk with him as soon as possible. The lady left the counter and went into a large back room in which I could see her through the glass window. After a little while, the receptionist returned telling me that Col. Shea had been on a special assignment for the past few months. No information about his assignment could be given out without special security clearance. She told me she would relay the message to him as soon as possible. In my mind, I was hoping that she would do that and he would call me as soon as he could. When I hit the road block of trying to find Col. Shea, I returned home. I was hoping I would arrive home before Keaton and Hannah returned. On the drive home I started thinking about what the receptionist said at the post locator. She said that Col. Shea was on a special assignment and that it was top secret. I couldn't help but wonder if that's what he was telling me when he came to my house. He said I couldn't say anything about it to anyone and that he called it the space force. I needed some answers, but I was afraid Keaton might be getting impatient. Hannah was working on her future and going off to college, but Keaton's future was in limbo and I was afraid he might do something irrational like making a decision and not thoroughly thinking it through. I knew as his mom, it was his future, his life. I wanted the decision to be fully and completely his. That is what Jack would have wanted also, but after he had become an astronaut and fixed the ozone layer and save the world. Then, Keaton could do whatever he wanted. I arrived home minutes before Keaton and Hannah. I asked them if they had a good day and they said yes. Keaton left after a short stay at home to take Hannah home because everyone seemed exhausted.

The next morning Keaton got up from a good night's rest. After breakfast, he proceeded to tell me about their trip to the University. He said it seemed to be a very nice place and that safety was no longer an issue. Jill said, "Why is Hannah's safety no longer an issue? They must have security guards or lights everywhere." Keaton said, "Well, not exactly. You see why I was talking to the registration office. I am thinking about registering for college there. I can look after Hannah and we can be together. I can also start my academic career." Jill replied, "It sounds like a good plan. You and Hannah have really thought it through." Keaton said, "Yes, we have talked about it a lot, but I would like to know what you think about it." "I just want you to be happy. What field of study would you be going in? What is your interest Keaton?" Jill asked. Keaton said, "To be honest, I still don't know, but I feel like I need to be moving in some direction, not just going in circles and spinning my wheels. Ever since I found the letter that dad put in the cubbyhole, I have not been able to get it off my mind. There is a fantasy world and a real world. Sometimes I think dad lived in a fantasy world, but this is a real world and we must make real world decisions. Therefore, I have decided to attend SMU with Hannah this fall." Jill said, "I am so proud of you for standing on your own two feet. I know that your father would be so proud of you, but Keaton, you didn't answer my question.

What field of study are you going in?" With an obnoxious look on Keaton's face, he said, "Geology/ Earth Science. Do you think dad would be pleased?" Jill had a faraway look on her face then she said, "I don't understand, but we seem to be headed in the right direction. At this point I don't know what the right direction is, but we are moving. When does the semester start and what about the finances? Are you sure they will accept you or have you been accepted already?" Keaton replied, "Well mom, this may sound weird, but when I was at the registrar's office to sign up for classes, they already had my name on the list. I don't know how they could have known my name. The information was all there and the fee for the courses were paid in full. Mom, I don't think you did this, but what about dad? Could he have done this before he died?" Jill sat down in the easy chair with her face in her hands saying, "I don't know son. I am confused. You know your father was not a religious man, but he did believe in God and that he was the creator of all things." "I know he did because dad prayed a prayer the first night we took the Numerator on the experimental try." Keaton said. Then, Jill said, "I think we need to pray for some divine guidance and understanding of the mysteries that neither one of us can figure out." After the words left Jill's mouth, someone knocked on the door. After our lengthy discussion over the past couple of hours, it was about noon time on Friday. Both Jill and Keaton went to the door to see who it was. It was Col. Shea. We all looked at each other as if what to say now. Jill finally invited Col. Shea into the house. He came in and sat down in the easy chair. Jill and Keaton sat across from him on the sofa. Col. Shea said, "I've heard you have been looking for me Mrs.

Ripper." Jill said, "Yes, that's right. You left me holding the bag for several months now." Keaton was confused with the conversation taking place, but he was not going to say anything at this point. Col. Shea said, "I have had a lot of hot irons in the fire as the old saying goes. There have been many meetings and discussions in which most of them I am not free to talk about, but as for you ma'am, the promises I made to you and Keaton have not been disregarded. In fact, that is why I am here today. The request you made to me has been approved, but with some guiding circumstances. If you and Keaton both agree to these guidelines, your objective can be achieved." "What are these guidelines?" Jill asked. Keaton interrupted and said, "what are you talking about promises, objectives, and guidelines? Would someone fill me in on what is going on." Jill went back and told Keaton about her previous meeting with Col. Shea. She also told him about her trip to Fort Bliss to find Col. Shea. At the time, he was gone with Hannah to SMU University. Col. Shea spoke up and said, "What did you find out at SMU?" Keaton first looked at his mom then looked at Col. Shea and said, "Suppose you tell us what you know about SMU and the earth science program." He replied, "So you found out about the pre-registration and the financial payments that have been given to the University on your behalf? This was all a part of the promise of the federal government and the president of the United States had made to your mom. If you decide not to attend SMU University the funds can be transferred to the University of your choosing. This University was chosen because of its location and its curriculum concerning earth science/ geology programs. The reason you were pre-registered at SMU is because the space force program is not ready for recruits of your stature. We the federal government assumed that you would want to be working toward your objective rather than waiting around doing nothing. The decision is yours to make, but after I was informed by you and your mother about what happened to your father, I told her I would investigate the circumstances to the best of my ability. In my research, I found a letter sent to the office of space research regarding Jack's belief in restoring the earth's ozone layer. While the letter was very vague in answers and seemed to be filled with biblical myth, the professors thought there were enough facts and truths in Jack's presentation to go forward and examine this myth. He also stated in his letter that Keaton would instruct you. The professors thought that Keaton might be able to assist them. Keaton said, "I'm sorry Col, but I don't know a thing about what you are saying and those plans you talk about are not mine. They are my dad's. So, will you please tell those professors that I cannot help them? Please tell them I am in the 12th grade trying to figure out my future." Col. Shea asked, "Have you ever seen the device that your dad made? He calls it the Numerator." "Yes, I have seen it, but I was younger than 10 years old and I didn't understand it then anymore than I do now." Keaton said. Col. Shea said, "I understand that, but these professors have no earthly idea as to what this Numerator your father made even looks like. Knowing what it looks like and how it works is a different thing." Then Keaton said, "I can go into the garage and get it if you would like to see it.

Then you would have as much knowledge as I do." Then Keaton yelled out to his mom and said, "Is dad's Numerator still in the garage?" While he was waiting for her to respond, he remembered that the people from the organization Free Will were supposed to come and clean out the garage of the donations in which they had given. Keaton's face went blank. "What's wrong Keaton?" Col. Shea asked. "I don't know if we still have it or not. Mom may have thrown it away." Keaton said. About that time there was a knock on the front door. Keaton was headed to the door to answer it and Jill, his mother was coming down the stairs to answer the door too. Before he answered the door, he asked his mom, "didn't you hear me calling for you?" Jill said, "No I didn't hear you." Keaton opened the door and Hannah stood there crying visibly upset. As Keaton reached to comfort her and Jill asked, "What's wrong Hannah?" Hannah was sobbing so badly that neither one of them understood what she was trying to say. Keaton said, "Sweet heart, what is wrong?" Hannah said, "My dad is missing and I have tried all morning to call you. Is your phone not working?" Hannah explained to Keaton, "Last night when you brought me home, my dad wasn't there. My mom and I thought they were having a late service and that he would be home shortly." Sometimes when Mr. Sosebee comes home late, he lies down on the sofa not wanting to disturb the rest of the family. When mom got up this morning she looked at Hannah and said he was not on the sofa. Hannah said, "We both have called and checked with everyone possible. The church pastor where he attended last night said service ended about 9:30 and Ron left promptly after the service to go home, he thought. My mom is hysterical and I am close behind her." Mrs. Ripper said, "I am so sorry for you and your mom, but I am sure things will be alright." Keaton then hopped in his Jeep and told Hannah, "I love you babe. I am going to look for your father." During the excitement, everyone seemed to forget about Col. Shea who is now standing in the foyer of the house. Jill saw him standing there and said, "I'm sorry Col. Shea, I hope you understand this meeting will have to continue at a later date." Col. Shea said, "I can certainly understand Mrs. Ripper and Hannah I am sorry to hear about your father." After Col. Shea had left, Jill got into the car with Hannah to go back to Hannah's house to help comfort her and her mother.

When they arrived at the Sosebee home, Keaton was there also. Sitting in the driveway, there were two patrol cars. One seemed to be a state vehicle and the other a county patrol car. Keaton was standing next to Hannah's mother as she was talking to the patrol officers. After a short conversation, a look of relief seem to come upon Mrs. Sosebee's face. Hannah got out of the car and ran towards her. When I arrived, Mrs. Sosebee was telling Hannah that her father had been in an accident, but was okay. They had taken him to the hospital during the night to check him out, but now he was ready to be released and come home. Keaton said, "I don't mind going to get him." Then Hannah said, "I will go with you and we will take my car. You know my dad doesn't like Jeeps" with a smile on her face. Then Keaton said, "Are you sure it's the Jeep that he doesn't like, maybe it is the driver" with a sarcastic look on his face. We were all glad things had worked out with Hannah's father. We were certainly glad that Mr. Sosebee was coming home. As things start to slow down, I wonder what happened to Col. Shea. I had forgotten all about him and his visit to the house that morning.

I remember calling out to mom wanting to find out if dad's Numerator was still there or if she had given it away to the Free Will society. Keaton interrupted his mother and Mrs. Sosebee talking in the driveway. He said, "I am sorry to interrupt, but mom what happened to Col Shea?" Jill answered him and said, "After Hannah came to the house with her news, I thought it was best to reschedule our meeting for a later date." Keaton said, "Great, that sounds like a plan. We can talk more about it tonight when we get home. Right now, I am going to the hospital with Hannah to see Mr. Sosebee. I will see you later."

After Jill left the Sosebee house and arrived home, she tried to call Col. Shea. When he answered his phone Jill told him that Mr. Sosebee had been in an accident, but was doing fine. She also told him that her and Keaton were sorry to have to leave so hastily and that she would like to reschedule their meeting as soon as possible. Col Shea told her that there was no need to apologize and that he understood their concern. He also told Jill that he would come back anytime at their convenience. Jill asked if he and his wife would be interested in coming over for dinner Friday night. Col Shea replied, "You don't have to do anything, but a home cooked meal sounds mighty tasty and to be honest, I don't have a wife. I suppose Jack never told you about the accident in which I lost my wife Cindy. If that changes your opinion about having me over for dinner, I understand. I do not want to impose upon you and Keaton at a family meal." Jill replied saying, "Jack always talked highly of you and I think he would be delighted to have you come to his house to have dinner with us. I will also invite Hannah to come have dinner with us this Friday. We will see you Friday night at 7 pm.

When Keaton got home that night, his mother told him about the phone conversation with Col. Shea. She told him to invite Hannah to dinner. Then Keaton said to his mom, "I have got to find that Numerator dad built because Shea wanted to see it." Jill said, "The last time I saw it was in the garage." "Wasn't that before the Free Will society came?" Keaton asked. "No, Keaton. I made sure they did not get it and some of the other things Jack wanted you to have." A couple of days had passed and Keaton went into the garage and started snooping around. He remembered his mom saying that she has kept dad's Numerator and some other things. Keaton's curiosity began to run in overdrive. He wondered what kinds of items his dad wanted him to have. Finally, he found his dad's Numerator inside a storage box that mom had bought and placed it in. There were some other items placed inside the storage box along with the Numerator, but Keaton had never seen anything like them before.

Keaton found a notepad with what seemed to be instructions. There was a crude picture that Jack had drawn of the Earth. There were rings around the outer surface of the Earth and a line pointing to a schematic diagram. Jack had written words pointing to the diagram with words like environment, outer layers, and firmaments. They did not mean anything to Keaton, but evidently everything to Jack. Keaton put the items back into the storage box to wait for Col. Shea. The week passed quickly and mom seemed to be edgy about Shea coming and I am sure I can understand why. Ever since dad had died, I have been the only male figure sitting at our kitchen table, but I am sure everything will be alright and she will be up to the test.

Col. Shea arrived right on time and mom's dinner was extraordinarily delicious. She had country fried chicken with all of the fixings. For dessert, she made a fresh peach cobbler. After the dinner, we went into the family room and while Col. Shea was holding his stomach, he began to speak stating, "That was a fine meal Mrs. Ripper." Mom spoke up and said, "I'm glad you liked it, but I wish you would call me Jill." Col Shea said, "Well, I think it would be more appropriate if you would call me Devin. My name is Col. Devin E Shea, but I would feel more at ease if you would call me Devin." Then mom nodded her head in agreement. Keaton said, "You know the items you wanted to see when you were here the last time? I will be right back. I am going to the garage to retrieve them."

Keaton was only gone a short period of time. When he arrived, he had the storage box with him. As he began to open the box, Col. Shea was looking over his shoulder to see what might be inside. When Keaton picked up the Numerator from inside the box, he told Col. Shea that the device his dad created is called "The Numerator."

It was the size of a small shoe box and weighed about 20 pounds. As Col. Shea reached over to touch the Numerator, he said, "I've never seen anything like it. What is it supposed to do?" Keaton then said, "When I was about eight years old, dad told me the Numerator counted part of the whole. I told dad at that time, I did not understand what he meant. Dad laughed at me and said I would understand when I got older. Col Shea, I am not eight anymore and I still don't understand what this Numerator does." Col Shea spoke up and said, "Neither do I, but maybe some of the professors at the University will enlighten both of us. Speaking of the University, I have some information to tell you and your mother. Is she close by?" Then Jill said, "I am right here" coming in from the kitchen where she had been cleaning up the dinner meal. Col Shea explained, "Keaton is enrolled and is supposed to start classes in the next couple of weeks at SMU University. The expenses have been paid for by the government. Keaton will receive advanced training in the Earth science career. When SMU feels that Keaton is ready for the next step in his career, he will then be assigned to a special unit in the United States space force academy. This special unit will be top secret. After a period of evaluation, Keaton will have the right to press forward or leave the space force with no strings attached. After he finishes his studies at SMU, he will be assigned to the US space force program. He will enter the program at the rank of second Lieut. After special training provided by the space program, Keaton will be ranked Captain. We anticipate this training to be accomplished as soon as possible. Mrs. Ripper, I want you to know this will be Keaton's decision. He may choose to withdraw from the program at any time. We do not have a list of the other candidates. Keaton's name was submitted to the president by his father Jack. Also alone with his name, the president was given instructions on how to repair our planet's ozone layer. Jack stated in his letter to the president that a Numerator had been built by him and that his son Keaton would have other materials available to assist in repairing the Earth's ozone layer. Col Shea said, "That is as much information that I can elaborate upon this time. Therefore, Keaton, I need your response to the request. I need your answer ASAP." Keaton looked at his mom and his mom looked at him. They both said,

"What would you do Devin?" He answered by saying, "You have been given a great test. One in which your father chose for you. You have been placed in an unusual situation, but if I had been given the opportunity, I would want to look back some day at my life and say I wish I had tried." Keaton said, "I just don't think I am able and more than that, I don't think I am capable. I don't understand how dad would think I could do something like this." Looking at Jill, Keaton said, "I don't want to let dad down. Therefore, I will do my best to achieve the objective. Whatever it may be." Col Shea answered and said, "I know you will do just fine and you will make both your mom and dad proud and the rest of the world will be astonished at your endeavors. In two weeks, you will start your training at SMU University. I will let all the parties involved know that operation Blue Deal is underway." Keaton interrupted and asked, "What do you mean by Operation Blue Deal?" Col Shea said, "That is the code word that your father suggested that we use for this world saving operation. Operation Blue Deal is an alternative for the corrupt politicians' plans called the New Green deal. After you start this training program, you will be sitting in on a lot of special meetings and many of your questions will be answered during these meetings. However, until then you must study and learn the goals of how to achieve our objectives. There has been a lot placed upon your shoulders, but I will be there every step of the way. Many other people have our backs. The whole world is pulling for you. Jill spoke up and asked, "Have you talked to Hannah about any of this?" Keaton said, "Yes mom, she knew I was going to be going with her to SMU, but as far as the space program, I did not know anything about it until tonight. Hannah and I still have lots to talk about." Jill said, Hannah, I hope you understand we love you and also consider you a big part of our family. We do not want you to feel left out." Hannah spoke up and said, "No, I am looking forward to going to school at SMU with Keaton. I plan to be by his side every step of the way, that is if Keaton wants me by his side." Keaton said, "Of course, but we have a lot to talk about, so I suppose I will take you home now. Col Shea, take care of yourself, I have a feeling we will be meeting very soon." Col Shea told Jill to take care of herself and to let him know if there was anything she needed help with.

It wasn't long until Keaton and Hannah were enrolled at SMU University. Many times during their commute Hannah and Keaton talked about their relationship. They both agreed that someday maybe in their future, they would possibly get married. They both agreed that they wanted to have two or three children. They both were brought up as an only child and they agreed that they did not want their children to be raised the same way. Keaton seemed to like and respect Hannah's parents a lot. He was glad that Mr. Sosebee was doing fine after his automobile accident. He did not want Hannah to have to go through life without her father figure. Sometimes during their commute to the university, they would talk about Keaton's father Jack. Keaton told Hannah, "I believe you would have liked him. He was a unique character. He was an ordinary man until the accident happened. After the accident, he was different. His life seemed to be more focused than just living. For example, in my life, I live day to day, but dad was focused on achieving the tasks that were at hand. I did not understand the objective that he wanted to achieve, but somehow I have gotten interwoven into his objective. Sometimes, I feel like I am not living my life to do what I want. I feel like I am living my life to fulfill dad's. Hannah spoke up and asked, "does that make you angry?" Keaton replied, "Well, I suppose that sometimes it does, but then again, I want my dad proud of me." Hannah said, "Maybe I can help you by using the Bible. The Bible says that Jesus came not into this world not to do his will, but the will of his father." Keaton said, "That is a fantastic analogy and it does help. You know, Col Shea said that I was the only candidate on the list and no other person could be chosen. He told me my father had chosen me and that I would be given knowledge and instructions on how to accomplish the task. The Bible said that Jesus prayed in the garden, "Father if it be thy will, let this cup pass from me, but not my will, but thy will be done." Therefore, if Jesus refused the world, the world would have lost its Savior."

Keaton arrived at SMU University. He walked up the official entrance known as the Boulevard. He had seen the band marching when watching the SMU football games. When Keaton first met with his guidance counselor, he was told he would be receiving instructions in the course of a Bachelors of Science in mechanical engineering along with a Bachelor of Science in physics. He was also informed that this course of instructions would normally be obtained in about 4 years but his course would be accelerated to less than six months. When he arrived home he told his mother, "I've got to get in touch with Col Shea." Jill told Keaton to call and talk to him directly. Col Shea answered the phone and could tell that Keaton was ecstatic. Col Shea said, "Settle down, I know what the professors must have sounded like an enormous task. I should have been there for you and I am sorry that I wasn't. I will be there tomorrow and you will understand it better."

The next day when Hannah and Keaton got to the university, Hannah left to go to her appointed classes and Keaton met Devin in the student Hall. Devin was carrying a briefcase which was handcuffed to his wrist. Keaton asked, "what is in the briefcase?" Col Shea said, "You will find out later." When they arrived at the physics lab Col Shea removed the briefcase and laid it on the table in front of them. When the professor entered the room, he seemed to be as confused about the situation as Keaton was. The professor said, "Hi, my name is Jeff Dockery and I am one of the professors here at SMU university. I was told by the president of the college to assist you in any way possible. So, with that being said, how can I help?" Col Shea spoke up and said, "I know professor Dockery that someone had to brief you. Have you heard anything about a special assignment called the New Blue Deal?" Professor Dockery said, "Yes I have, but I have been ordered not to say anything to you until the codeword was mentioned. May I look inside the briefcase?" As he was unlocking the briefcase Keaton and Devin were looking anxiously to see what was inside. There was a notepad that seemed to be handwritten. There was also an eyeglass case. When the professor removed the notepad from the briefcase he asked Keaton, "Have you ever seen this notepad before?" Keaton answered the professor by saying, "No sir." As he took a closer look, he said, "I think the handwriting on the tablet matches the handwriting of my father Jack." The professor said, "That is good Keaton, you are exactly right.

This is a tablet your father left behind with instructions on how to build these eye glasses and that if anyone else tried to wear these glasses, other than you Keaton, they would go blind." Col Shea said, "what are you supposed to do professor?" Professor Dockery replied and said, "Well to be honest with you, we were afraid to try them on with the warning Jack described. Jack called them the retainer glasses and if Keaton read with them on, he would instantly retain the information for the rest of his life. He also stated that while he was making these glasses, he briefly glanced through one of the lenses and his eyes were never closed after." Keaton said, "that's the truth. Dad's eyes were never closed. He never blinked and mom said he slept with his eyes open. Mom and I noticed his eyes, but we never talked about it or mentioned it to dad." The professor said, "would you be interested in an experiment with the glasses or are you afraid to put the glasses on?" Keaton said, "We have come too far to stop now and my dad is not a liar. I trust him." The professor then wrote scientific formulas on the Blackboard that were highly complex. Only a well resource scientist would understand the complexity of these formulas. He told Keaton to read the formulas and the black board will then be flipped to the other side. I am the only one with 30 years of scientific training that can write these formulas. Are you ready to proceed with this experiment?" Col Shea said, Keaton, I told you and your mother you can withdraw from the project at any time. I am telling you as a friend and a friend of your dad's that you do not have to proceed with this experiment." Keaton said, "I appreciate you Col Shea and you are a friend, but these glasses were designed by my dad specifically for me. I am willing to put the glasses on and proceed with this experiment." The Professor reached into the briefcase and removed the eyeglass case and told Keaton to hold them. He was not to remove them until he was told. The professor then went and wrote on the Blackboard using his notes from the scientific formulas. After the professor had written the formulas he told Keaton to get ready to read the notes that he had written. As Professor Dockery was flipping the black board, Keaton removed the glasses from the eyeglass case and put them on. Keaton read the scientific formulas to himself and immediately the professor turned the black board over again. This time, Keaton had removed his eyeglasses and returned them to the case. Professor Dockery came to the table in which Keaton and Shea were sitting. He took out his notepad which he had used to write on the Blackboard and told Keaton to explain the scientific formula that he had written on the Blackboard. Keaton explained the formula in a very discreet and professional manner. He never hesitated to describe the formula. It was as if he was a 12th grader learning to say his ABCs. Both the professor and Shea could not believe what they were witnessing, hearing, or seeing. Professor Dockery said, "There is no way that a freshman student could remember the formula written on the black board." They both looked at Keaton and asked, "How do you feel?" Keaton said, "I feel fine, so when do we get started?" Col Shea asked about Keaton's eyes. Keaton replied, "I am fine and my dad is a hero. I think dad received a gift from God and wanted to share it with me. In fact, I think he wanted to share it with the whole world. What a man my dad was and what a gift he received."

Immediately after the experiment, professor Dockery started gathering literature describing the overall objective. Keaton started reading the literature with unsurpassed enthusiasm. Keaton took a few short moments away from the literature to tell Shea goodbye.

Shea left the building shaking his head and telling professor Dockery, "he is now in your hands." Keaton's training went on for weeks. It was mainly Professor Dockery, but the other staff members and professors would assist in Keaton's training. Keaton also received training from other local universities. He received a degree in natural resource management from Park University at Fort Bliss Texas that focused on practical utilization of Natural Resources as well as sustainability issues. He also received a bachelor's degree from Baylor University that focused on environmental health science. With all this training that Keaton had received for the past six months, he was still himself. It did not change his personality or his sense of humor. Keaton said that all the training that he had received from the universities, he had not retained. He remembered the prime objective. Keaton said, "Now I understand the problem, but knowing how to fix the problem is another question."

It was almost Christmas time, a very special time of the year. After Christmas is over, we will start a new year and in a few short weeks after that, Keaton would be going to Florida to start his space Force training. There seemed to be a lot on the agenda. The next few months would be no different than the last few months. Things are really building up, but Keaton seemed to be up for the task. It was time to go home and to be with his mom and Hannah for Christmas. Everyone seemed to be excited just to spend some quality time with one another. Keaton was anxious to eat another Christmas dinner, but couldn't help but think about our last dinner that he had. Col Shea had come over and told us to start calling him Devin. I will never forget that it was also the night I made my commitment to join the space force academy. A lot has happened over the past few months and who can guess what the future may hold. Keaton said, "I want to spend some time with Hannah because things got very hectic at school and we were not able to commute together for many days. I hope her studies are going well. She was studying to be a psychologist. I told her one time that dad could have used her, but now I am wondering if I am the one that needs her. I know I need her and I hope she still wants and needs me. I wonder if Devin might come over during Christmas. I think he and mom have a lot in common. They both enjoy each other's company and they have a lot to talk about. I am not trying to be a matchmaker, but even the Bible said it is not good for a man to be alone. I miss my dad and I wish he was still around, especially this time of year. I have fond memories of him that I will cherish for the rest of my life."

It was long about Thanksgiving time when I began to think about how blessed I was. I have a mom that really loves me and cares for me. I also have a girlfriend that I love with all of my heart and I want her some day to be my wife. So I went looking the other day to buy her an engagement ring at the jewelry store and I found her a beautiful ring that I want to give her some time during this Christmas season. It has got to be the right time and the atmosphere has got to be right.

On Christmas Eve while waiting on Santa to arrive, Keaton and Jill were also waiting for Hannah to come over. Someone knocked at the door and I knew it wasn't Hannah because Hannah never knocks. Jill went to the door to see who it was and it was Shea. Mom said, "Come in Devin. What brings you out this way on Christmas Eve?" Devin said, "I was sitting at the house when I suddenly realized that I never paid you back for that wonderful meal you made a few months ago. Have you eaten yet?" Keaton and Jill looked at one another and said, "No, we are waiting for Hannah to arrive." Devin said, "Okay good, may I be excused?" Devin turned around in the foyer and went back out the door to his car. He looked as if he was retrieving something from inside. Hannah pulled up in the driveway behind Col Shea and asked, "Can I help you?" Hannah and Col Shea remove the items from the car and take them into the house. Once they are inside, they place the pizzas and sodas on the table. Devin said, "I know it doesn't look like much compared to the meal that Jill prepared. I am not much of a cook, but I hope you like pizza." The four of us sat down at the table and began consuming the pizza. Jill told Devin that it was very nice of him to bring the pizzas but that he didn't owe her anything. After eating, Keaton asked Hannah if she would like to go for a drive. Hannah replied, "I don't know if I should be riding around with a stranger. We haven't seen each other in months. Everyone at the table laughed at her comment as they were getting up from the table.

Kenan Hannah drove to City Park in El Paso. Keaton said, "I want to show you something. My dad brought me here when I was eight years old. He showed me his Numerator and how it worked. He said that one day it might save the world. I want you to stand right here." Keaton got down on one knee and pulled out a small box from his pocket. "Open it." He told Hannah. When she began to open the box, she was laughing and then began to cry. Hannah said, "Why did you do this? I didn't expect anything till after you have achieved your father's objective." Keaton said, "I love you Hannah before the objective, during the objective, and after the objective. It has no bearings on my love for you. This is only an engagement ring, we do not have to set a date for the wedding, but I was afraid if I did not put a ring on your finger, some other bachelor might come and steal you away." After a few sweet kisses, Hannah and Keaton could hardly wait to get back home and tell their parents. Hannah's mom and dad were so excited. They said Keaton becoming their future son-in-law was a great Christmas gift. Keaton's mom was also excited. The thought of Hannah becoming her daughter-in-law was a dream come true. Jill said she knew that there was something up when Keaton asked Hannah to go for a drive. She felt like Keaton wanted to be alone with Hannah.

After the holidays had passed, the countdown is on. Very soon Keaton would be leaving for Cape Canaveral Florida. He would be starting his Advanced Training in the United States space force. Everyone seemed very excited about his upcoming training, but they were also sad to know that he would be leaving to go to Florida. Hannah told Keaton she would write to him every day, but she didn't expect him to write to her quite as often because of his busy training. Keaton told his mom and Hannah that he would write to them as often as possible. Shea was already at Port Canaveral waiting for Keaton's arrival on March 13th. When Keaton arrived at the post, he was immediately sworn in as a Cadet for the US space force. He was also given his uniform in the rank of second lieutenant. The command center of the US space force knew that these procedures were very unorthodox, but Lieutenant Keaton was an unorthodox cadet. His mission was very clear that he had to save the world. The Earth's ozone layer was getting thinner and would quite possibly disappear in a few more years. Keaton's mission was to restore the Earth's ozone layer because without the ozone layer protecting the Earth from the deadly ultraviolet rays, all of life on Earth could possibly be destroyed. After Lieutenant Keaton was taken on a tour of Cape Canaveral, he was taken to his quarters where he would stay, sleep, and rest until his training had been completed. Keaton was very excited to be at Cape Canaveral because he had read a lot of material concerning it. Merritt Island was part of the region known as Space Coast and that is where all of the previous astronauts were launched into space. Keaton hadn't been there a day until he started thinking about Hannah and wondering what she was doing. He was thinking to himself that the training back at SMU University was more about training the mind, but the training at Port Canaveral will be more Hands-On and physical. Keaton said, "I can remember my dad saying you need book learning, but you also need a lot of common sense. I have had the book learning, hopefully I will be getting the common sense training." Keaton hadn't been at Port Canaveral for a couple of weeks when Shea came by the quarters to visit. Shea told Keaton that he knew he had been very busy and that he was just trying to stay out of his way. Shea had two other officers with him that were both in the space Force program together. He introduced them both as Lieutenant Colby and Lieutenant Trenton. Devin told me they had been cadets at the Academy now for about 2 years. After shaking Trenton's and Colby's hand, they both wanted to assure me that they would be there to help me to achieve my objective in any way that they could. As they were leaving, Keaton said, "I appreciate your help and the Lord knows because I am scheduled for my first space flight in the simulator tomorrow." Lieutenant Colby spoke up and said, "How long have you been here?" Keaton replied and said, "About two weeks." Lieutenant Trenton said, "It was almost a year before I got to see the space flight simulator." Col Shea interrupted and said, "Well, Lieutenant Keaton is not an ordinary cadet. He comes with unprecedented credentials in which neither of us are free to speak of at this time. Keaton will welcome any insight that you might be willing to share with him, but as far as his training objective, I believe the less spoken of it, the better off we will all be. It is not an order, it is a request." The other Lieutenants said, "Yes sir" and the three of them departed the quarters.

When Keaton arrived at the flight simulator, Shea was there to meet him. Lieutenants Colby and Trenton were also there. They were talking to a man dressed in a white jumpsuit. They introduced the man to Lieutenant Keaton. His name was senior space flight instructor James Burton. Mr. Burton said, "So, you are Lieut. Keaton? I have been looking forward to meeting you. Is it okay if I call you Keaton?" Keaton said, "I have been called that my whole life." All of the men chuckled and Mr. Burton said, "The space flight simulators do a great job mimicking reality however, only to a certain point. They can trick your body into feeling like you're experiencing turbulence and take advantage of how your inner ear senses acceleration. A flight simulator must provide the astronaut like you, Keaton with as closeness in relation to the space light as possible on Earth. The requirements for the realization increases with the complexity of the situation. For example, when the astronaut fires the thrusters, the simulator must activate readouts and lights showing the thrusters firing, fuel reducing, velocity changes, and show movement in the scenes outside the cabin window. This is flight simulator 271. It is a spacecraft cabin suspended on Hydraulics enabling it to tilt. It gives the astronauts a true space flight example. You will also be training in a centrifuge which creates artificial g-forces. You will also be learning specialized breathing and muscle tension techniques. Specialized outfits will have air bladders to constrict the legs and the abdomen during High G's to keep blood in the upper body. Lieutenant Keaton, are you ready for your first space flight simulator run?" Keaton left to go put on the necessary equipment before the space flight simulator. After he left the area, the space flight instructor asked Shea, "did you see his face sir?" Shea shook his head and said, "No, why sir?" Mr. Burton said, "his face looked strange and I don't think he even blinked his eyes." Col Shea started thinking about the past. After a few moments Keaton returned wearing his space suit. Col Shea asked, "Keaton, how do you feel?" Keaton answered and said, "I feel fine Devin, I mean Col Shea" with a smile on his face. After the training session was over, he exited the flight simulator all in smiles and a thumbs up.

After several more weeks of extreme intensive training, Keaton's flight instructor Mr. James told Shea that Keaton seemed to look exhausted from extensive training. Instructor James Burton told Shay that he thought it would do Keaton a world of good to go home for Easter weekend. Shea agreed with James and told Keaton that he had a three-day furlough for the upcoming Easter weekend. Keaton was delighted to get to go home and see his mom and his girlfriend Hannah. Hannah had written to Keaton just about every day. The days she did not write to him were the days she called him. The day before Keaton left to go home, they reminded him not to do anything stupid that would cause him to get hurt. Col Shea said, "You know if you do anything stupid, it would jeopardize your upcoming mission? You are irreplaceable. If you get hurt, the mission would have to be scrubbed." Keaton acknowledged what Shea was saying. He said, "Will you be coming over for Easter dinner?" Devin replied, "No, I have several important meetings that require my attendance."

When Keaton arrived back home at El Paso International Airport, Hannah was there to meet him. The drive back to the Rippers home was only about 45 minutes from the airport. As they were traveling, they asked each other what they had been doing. Keaton said, "I want to know all about your studies." Hannah said, "I will tell you all about it later, but right now, I want to know how the space force academy is going." Keaton replied, "It is going great as far as I know." Hannah asked Keaton, "How is Col Shea? Will he be joining us for Easter dinner?" Keaton explained, "I asked him to come, but he said he had some important meetings to attend that would require his presence." "How is my mom?" Keaton asked. "She is doing fine, but I think she will be a little disappointed that Devin will not be joining us for dinner. I think your mom likes him more than you realize." Hannah explained. This time they're pulling into the Ripper's driveway. Jill met Hannah at the front door and while hugging her neck she said, "Where is my handsome astronaut at?" She removed her arms from around Hannah's neck and tackled Keaton. She threw her arms around his neck. Jill was so excited to have Keaton back home for a couple of days. He had never been away from home for any kind of extended time. Neither had she lived by herself even before her and Jack had gotten married. When she removed her arms from Keaton's shoulders she asked, "Where is Devin? I bet he is not coming. That is his problem, I guess he won't get any of my homemade peach cobbler." Keaton spoke up and said, "He wanted to come, but he had important business to attend to." Jill told Keaton, "Well, I want to hear about your training. Tell me about Florida. Your father and I always planned on taking a trip to Florida, but we never got the chance to go." Keaton said, "It is a beautiful state. They have great beaches everywhere. The people are very nice and the girls are beautiful, but none of them can match up to my beautiful Hannah. It is good to be home because there is no place like it here. Just like Dorothy said in the movie Wizard of Oz "there's no place like home."

After relaxing for a bit, Keaton went out to check his Jeep. He told his mother that his Jeep needed to be driven. The jeep had been sitting there for a while and it had not been driven. Keaton and Hannah went for a drive and his Jeep. They drove to see Hannah's parents. Her parents were doing great and pleased to see Keaton. They told Keaton they had been praying for him. The Sosebee's were a very religious family. Mr. Sosebee spoke to Keaton and said, "I hope your training has been going well. How do you like Florida?" Before Keaton could answer his question, Mr. Sosebee said "I took my family there to Disney World in Orlando several years ago. We had a wonderful time didn't we Hannah? Have you told him about our trip to Florida?" "No, I haven't been around Keaton lately to talk to him about much of anything" said Hannah. Hannah told her mom and dad she would be back later because she left her car at the Ripper's. "I will see you both later, take care of yourself" Keaton said to the Sosebee's. Mr. Sosebee said, "Take care of yourself and our daughter." He then started talking about Florida again as Hannah and Keaton were exiting the front door. On the way back to Keaton's house, Hannah spoke up and said, "I guess you noticed my father has a touch of Alzheimers. I am not going to criticize him for repeating himself because he cannot help it. This disease is affecting his memory." Keaton said, "There is no need to apologize. Your father is a good man. He is not as young as he once was and getting older is something we will have to deal with one day."

The next day was Easter and they had a wonderful dinner. Keaton got to relax and watch football. He also spent time with his mother and Hannah. He shared with them some of his experiences at the space force program. He told them about his instructor James Burton and how much of a character he was. He mentioned the other Cadets Lieut. Cold and Lieut. Trenton. The hours were slipping away because tomorrow he would be leaving to go back to Cape Canaveral, Florida. Hannah would not be able to take him to the airport because she had an important test at the University. Jill would be sending him off at the airport.

When Keaton arrived back in Florida, Col. Shea was waiting to greet him. He said, "It's good to have you back Keaton. I hope everything is good at home and you had a good weekend." Keaton said, "Yes sir, I wish you could have been there." Col Shea said, "We have a lot of things to talk about and there are some other people I would like for you to meet." He introduced me to Captain Rylee, Lieut Downs and Lieut Massey. Col Shea told me that they were assisting me in the New Blue Deal project. Keaton knew the Blue Deal was code for restoring the Earth's ozone layer. Keaton said, "How much do they know about the deal?" Col Shea explained, "They have been briefed and I suppose they know as much as I do at this point. Captain Rylee and his assistant Lieut Downs are in charge of the Lunar Space rover called Clean Sweep. It is a space rover which is designed similar to a hypervac or a regenerative airvac streets sweeper. The plans or design of the Lunar Space rover were given to the space administration by your father before his passing. Lieut Massey has been training and given the responsibility to maintain five cylindrical shape objects which will be used to contain over 50,000 lbs each of the lunar surface firmament. These designs were also found in your father's notes. You three will be working closely together and you will have to depend on each other during this mission. I suggest you spend as much time together learning about each other. The mission is scheduled for the month of July and yes, that is this year. I'm not going to ask if you have any questions because that is all we have at this point. Keaton reached out to shake hands with his fellow New Blue Deal comrades and teammates.

They did have a lot to talk about. They tried to get to know each other. They began to tell each other where they were from and why they joined the US space force. It seemed as though everyone was chosen because of some special ability that they must have had. After spending a few days together and going over our special projects, Col Shea thought it would be beneficial for us to take a few days and travel. We studied the colleague of planetary analogues and decided that a trip to the plains of Atacama Desert in Northern Chile in South Peru might be interesting. It is much like the lunar surface and void of life living organisms. We also went to Cinter Lake in Northern Arizona because that is where a lot of Apollo astronauts trained back in the 60's. While seeing these places might have been helpful and interesting, I think Shea knew that spending time with one another was more important than the sightseeing tour. When we got back to the space force complex, the crew began to settle in on achieving their specialized assignments. Keaton had been given the command of the Space Shuttle known as the shuttle of Hope. The name Hope was given to this special spacecraft because it is the Hope For All Mankind. The Earth has five layers of the atmosphere. The Troposphere, Stratosphere, Mesosphere, Thermosphere, and the Exosphere. The ozone layer exists between the second and third layer. Keaton will fly the space shuttle Hope between the Stratosphere and Mesosphere. He will release the lunar surface firmaments that Captain Rylee and Lieut Downs have gathered. After the firmaments have been released from the cylindrical capsule,

Keaton will return and retrieve another full capsule dispersing them until all canisters are empty. The scientists are hoping that the firmament from the lunar moon surface will restore the Earth's ozone layer. They are also hoping that 5 canisters will be enough firmament particles to completely circle and cover the Earth's ozone layer. Col Shea said, "I was informed by some of our leading scientists that people on the Earth will be able to track Keaton's travel as he circles the Earth, much like we can see a jet's aircraft vapor. When it's hot, humid, exhaust from the jet engine mixes with the earth atmosphere or as simple as an old crop-dusting plane releasing its dust on a field of corn. As all of you know this is an experiment and nothing like this has ever been attempted before, but who knows it might just work. Who would have thought that a piece of moldy bread would bring about the discovery of penicillin." Keaton said, "I feel a little more informed and relaxed now about our upcoming mission. After hearing Col Shea's lecture and spending time with the new blue deal space crew, I am ready to repair the Earth's ozone layer sir." Shea then explained that when we spray the lunar firmament or space dust into the ozone layer and it mixes with the atmospheric gasses that make up the ozone layer, the damaged holes in the ozone layer should be repaired. It's like patching a hole in a sheetrock wall using sheetrock mud. Lieut Downs spoke up and said, "Col Shea, how long do you expect the repair work to last, if it does work?" Shea said, "The Earth's ozone layer did just fine until we, I mean all of mankind, started putting those dangerous man-made chemicals and chlorofluorocarbons into our atmosphere. In the beginning, I believe this earth was made perfect. The biblical review of

God creating the heavens and the Earth God stated that it was good after he finished each project of that day and I believe the Earth's ozone layer was perfect also.

Maybe after our repair job is completed, it might be perfect again. Soon the days, weeks, and even months were passing by rapidly. The training schedule seemed to be right on time. On July 1st, Col Shea informed the new blue deal members of a special event coming up. On July 4th, also known as Independence Day, we will be having a party called Restoring Eden. Col Shea said, "Your family and friends will be invited as our guest. The Space Force Academy is proud to sponsor this extraordinary event. We will have dignitaries from across the nation and the world. Political leaders in positions as high as presidential are expected to be in attendance. There will also be celebrities from the sports and movie industry coming to the party." Lieut Keaton said, "Great, it is cool that all of these people will be coming. What about my girlfriend Hannah?" Col Shea said with a smirk on his face, "I don't know about her. I have heard through the grapevine that she is engaged to some nice looking astronaut and that he is a member of the new blue deal space crew." Keaton jokingly threw his arms up in the air, shook his head, and walked away.

July 4th finally arrived and the party known as Restoring Eden was underway. People from all over the world are coming to this event. While Keaton was excited to see all of the digitaries, there was only one plane he was most excited about. Flight number 217 from El Paso, Texas. This plane carried Hannah, Jill, and the Sosebee's. Keaton and Hannah spent the day together and she was introduced to all of Keaton's friends and crew members. They shook hands with Presidents, Governors, Senators, and politician leaders from around the world, but they just wanted to spend time alone. When it was the end of the party, the commander of the Space Force operation center made an announcement, "Congratulations to the members and the staff of the new blue deal space force crew. After receiving information from all departments, training is completed. The Space Force administration has set a lunch date for July 21st. They also gave all throttle up to the mission Restoring Eden." Keaton looked at his mom and Hannah and said, "That is only 17 days out, but tomorrow is July 5th. I hope they won't schedule any training sessions for us tomorrow." At about the same time Keaton was talking to his mom and Hannah, a voice came over the loudspeaker saying, "This is Captain Liana scheduling supervisor for the new blue deal project Restore Eden space crew. Attention all members of the blue deal space crew will report to Major Johnson at 0500 hours tomorrow in Building 927. This is a muster roll call all crew members will be expected with no exceptions." Keaton looked at his mom and Hannah and said, "Well there goes our Sunday dinner." Jill said, "It's okay son, our plane is scheduled to depart at 9:40 in the morning anyways. I guess we will have to say our goodbyes tonight." Keaton said, "Why do we have to say our goodbyes tonight? Captain Liana said that the roll call would not be until 0500 hours in the morning. I have at least six or seven more hours to spend with Hannah before it is time." Hannah said, "No Keaton, that is not a good idea. You need your rest. We have had a good day and I will call you when we get back to El Paso." They kissed and then Keaton said his goodbyes.

One day during our q-and-a session, Captain Rylee said, "Sir I have a question that has been on my mind for some time now. The lunar firmament's or space dust, what makes it different from that of the Earth?" "That's a very good question. That is something I asked myself several months ago. I began talking to one of the college professors and he explained it this way to me. The professor said soil can become extinct or in other words dead. When Farmers keep harvesting from a particular field year after year, they will eventually remove all the nutrients from soil which makes the soil infertile with no nutrients. A farmer would diagnose his field and fertilize it with a necessary product to increase the soil's nutrients. We know that the ozone layer is damaged which is why this diagnosis arrived many years ago. Some scientists say with time, the ozone layer will repair itself, but other scientists strongly disagree with their analysis. Keaton's father invented an apparatus called the Numerator. This machine is said to count the nutrients in the soil. Almost all of the soil on Earth is contaminated from people and other living organisms. Jack believed that the soil or the firmaments on the lunar surface will be free from these contaminants, making it an ideal product to repair the Earth's ozone layer. One of your first assignments is to find out if Jack's numerator is accurate in his assumption of the lunar firmaments." Col Shea said, "Rylee, I hope that answers your question. Does anyone else have a question?" Lieut Massey asked, "Yes… Can we all go eat now? I am starving." With a smile and chuckle, they all said, "Certainly" and left for the dining hall.

The commander of the space force agency gave a special interview to all news outlets and agencies. His comments were that time is swiftly passing for the launch of the Space Shuttle known as Clean Sweep. Captain Rylee and Lieut Downs are scheduled to arrive in approximately two weeks and they will arrive at the lunar space station known as the peak of eternal life on the moon's South Pole. Other members of the space force new blue deal Spaceteam have already arrived. Captain Rylee along with the rest of the new blue deal crew will begin immediately to collect the lunar firmaments and fill the five cyclical shaped canisters. Each of these canisters will weigh around 50,000 pounds. Four canisters will be stored at the space station circling the Earth allowing Lieut Keaton easy access to the full canisters after he has emptied and dispersed his first full canister. Lieut Massey will be in charge of transporting the canisters from the lunar surface and maintaining them at the Earth's Space Station. Lieutenant Keaton will arrive three days after the first party has already arrived and accomplished their task. After one solar night of the lunar surface, Lieutenant Keeton will proceed with his historic mission to repair the Earth's ozone layer. The space Force Commander ended his briefing by saying he would not take any questions at this time. He made a statement telling the Press court that any information printed or released not covered in his briefing would be considered a break in our national security. The person or organization would be penalized to the fullness of the law. The commander proceeded by saying any individual or news agency breaking the code of security would be barred with a lifetime ban of all future briefings. He ended the announcement again by saying I will not answer any questions. The next briefing is scheduled for July 21st at 0800 hours, have a good day.

After the Commander's briefing, Col Shea's appearance seemed to change. He headed straight for the Commander's office and upon entering Shea said, "Commander Johnson, may I have a word with you?" "Yes, by all means. What is on your mind?" asked Commander Johnson. Col Shea said, "Have I been intentionally or accidentally misinformed about our mission sir?" Commander Johnson responded with a sharp tone and said, "Col Shea, what do you mean by a change in our mission?" Col Shea said, "I was not informed that Lieut Keaton would be going to the moon and staying overnight on the lunar surface. The last information I received was that Lieut Keaton would be rendezvous with Lieut Massey at our space station. I did not know he would be going to the moon first then coming back to our space station." Commander Johnson replied in a calm voice, "I am sorry, but sometimes things change. I am sorry you did not get the message, but the truth is, Lieut Massey's space shuttle is not equipped to carry the lunar hypervac modified space rover from the lunar surface to the space station. The space shuttle known as Hope is the only space shuttle that is equipped to transport the hypervac and canisters full of firmaments. The hyper back not only retrieves the lunar firmaments, but it also disperses these firmaments in the Earth's ozone layer, much like a house vacuum or a Shop-Vac. They can suck in particles or they can blow out particles." Col Shea said, "So what you're saying is that Lieut Keaton will be transporting both the hypervac and 50,000 pound canister of firmaments from the moon's surface to the ozone layer? I must highly protest and criticize this last-minute change to our mission. We have less than two weeks before our next scheduled briefing and according to my understanding, I was told in order to keep the public and the rest of the United States adversaries at bay, the first stage of our mission the new blue deal was scheduled to launch at the same precise time you are giving your July 21st briefing at 0800 hours." Commander Johnson explained, "You are right. The mission of the new blue deal is still on schedule. The first launch will be July 21st at 0800 hours." Col Shea said, "That does not give us much time Commander." "I understand Col Shea, may I suggest that you get busy. If Lieut Keaton is not aware of these changes, I suggest you inform him. Have a great day." Commander Johnson said.

Col Shea left immediately looking for the crew members of the new blue deal. As he located them at different parts of the training facility, he informed them of a 3:00 meeting at the hangar deck number 5. As the crew members began to arrive shortly before 3, the enthusiasm and the excitement of the upcoming mission was alive and well. When Col Shea walked into the hangar deck, the chatter quickly ceased when someone hollered "Attention." As Col Shea reached the podium, he told the flight crew members to be at ease. He also told the crew members to listen closely as he read the schedule out loud. For the next couple of weeks, if you do not concur with the upcoming events please stand. If there is no one standing after I read the schedule, the meeting will be adjourned. You will be acknowledging and concurring with the upcoming events. If there is anyone standing after my reading of the schedule, we will proceed to discuss any issue. At the end of the meeting, no one was standing. This confused Col Shea. He makes a statement questioning, "So, everyone here acknowledges and concurs with the upcoming schedule?" The crew of the new blue deal were synchronized. Col Shea thought to himself, "I must have been the only person to not get the memo. I am glad Lieut Keaton was informed." That night Keaton could not sleep. I guess he had a lot on his mind thinking about the upcoming mission. He was also thinking about Hannah, hoping that she, Jill, and the rest of the family were doing okay. However, the biggest thing that was on his mind was the lie that he had told when Shea had the 3:00 meeting, talking about the upcoming schedule and wanted to make sure that everyone was on the same page. Keaton was not aware of the changes, but didn't want to jeopardize or delay the upcoming mission. After Keaton realized that he could not sleep around 2:00 in the morning he called Col Shea. When he answered the phone, the first thing he said was "Can't sleep Keaton?" Keaton said, "How did you know sir?" Col Shea replied, "Because, I could not sleep either. I knew you were lying today on the hangar deck. I kept saying to myself, "How can he know?" Keaton said, "I did not want to jeopardize or postpone our mission." Col Shea said, "That is very noble and stupid of you. What were you going to do when you found out you had to go to the moon? Were you going to fake it? That would have put the mission at risk for failure." Keaton pleaded, "I know sir, but what are we going to do now?" Col Shea paused and said, "Well… since the truth is out, I am going to get some sleep and I suggest you do the same. I will see you in the morning at my office at 0700 hours. Bring your glasses with you, I have a strong feeling you are going to need them."

When Keaton arrived at Col Shea's office, he was already there awaiting his arrival. Keaton and Shea started to work immediately because they both knew there was no time to waste. Shortly after they started working, Keaton said, "Col Shea, I am sorry I lied to you. I was wondering if I was the only one who lied. Did the rest of the crew know about the changes?" "Yes, Lieut Keaton, they all knew. I made several phone calls this morning. Captain Rylee, Lieut Downs, and Lieut Massey assured me that they were all aware of the changes. You and I had not received information of the changes yet. Did you bring the special glasses that your dad made you?" Col Shea asked. Keaton told him yes and placed the eyeglasses on the table. Col Shea asked, "Have you been using these glasses?" Keaton jokes, "I wouldn't leave home without them." After Keaton had to read the prescribed procedures, he removed the glasses and placed them back in the case. Col Shea asked him "what do you think?" Keaton blinked his eyes a couple of times and put his right forefinger under his chin and said, "this is a walk in the park. It is a piece of cake." Col Shea said, "that is reassuring. I thank God that your father Jack was given this vision. I hope that after this mission is over, he will receive the honors due to him." Keaton agreed and said, "He was a great man and a good father to me." Day by day and hour by hour the whole team kept rehearsing the events that would be taking place on the moon's surface and stratosphere of the Earth. The enthusiasm was very high for the upcoming mission. On July 16th the new blue deal crew had a meeting on the hangar deck number five. The crew members were sitting around a table talking about the upcoming mission, when Col. Shea entered the hangar and told them to keep their seats. Col. Shea went to the table and placed an object about the size of a shoebox. He asked the crew members if they knew what the object was. Everyone was looking around when Keaton raised his arm signifying that he knew what it was. Keaton had written words on the outside of the box. Jack's toy honor or disgrace to God be the glory. Col Shea said, "This is the Numerator that Keaton's father invented before he passed away. The Numerator along with other inventions by Jack have brought us to this point in time. Captain Rylee will be taking the Numerator on board the first shuttle flight. He is in charge of determining if the moon's firmaments will recharge the Earth's ozone layer, before the lunar space rover called Clean Sweep is put into action. If the Numerator's count of the moon's firmament is below 90%, the rest of the mission will be scrubbed and awarded. Does anyone have a question at this time?" Lieutenant Rylee raised his hand and said, "I am honored to be chosen for this task and mission, but I do have one lingering question. If the lunar firmament is below 90% and the mission is scrubbed, what is the amount of the firmaments in the Earth's ozone layer now?" Col Shea said, "That is a very good question. I don't think I can answer your question. Tests have been made in different parts of the Earth in which the numerator has traveled. Many scientists have tested the soil using the numerator and multiple different places on our planet. However, the highest percent was discovered on a Barren island off the coast of Canada and it was only 75% using the numerator. Therefore, if Jack's theory of the moon's firmaments is not correct, this project will go down in disgrace and not honor. Lieut Keaton rose to the floor and said, "I have a few words. Jack was my father. No other person in this room knew him except for Col Shea. When I was eight years old, Captain Shea was my father's company command. My father was in an accident. It occurred while he was serving in the military. The accident was never publicized, but my father's life changed drastically. He started having visions, talking about space and the Earth's ozone layer. He also changed physically because he never closed his eyes. He felt that what happened to him was a gift from God. My dad then built the Numerator and left other schematic diagrams for future inventions. I don't know if my dad's inventions will prove honor or disgrace. I do know that long ago there was an explorer that believed the Earth was round and he discovered the New World." At the end of his statement, Keaton sat down. It was a breathtaking show of unity because the new blue deal crew stood up showing gratitude and jubilation. The enthusiasm of the mission was higher than ever. Col Shea knew that was good because the first flight with Captain Rylee and Lieut Downs was scheduled to blast off from Cape Canaveral at 0800 hours on July 21st.

It was Saturday July 21at 0600 hours. Col Shea and Lieut Keaton were standing in in the launchpad 39B at port Canaveral nicknamed the milk stool. It was the same place where the space rocket Apollo had launched headed to the moon. It is also the same place where the space shuttles Challenger, Discovery, Atlantis, Columbia, and the Endeavor had launched from. At 0800 hours, Captain Rylee and Lieut Downs would head to the moon, initiating the start of the mission known as the new blue deal. At the same time, commander Johnson will be holding a media briefing at an adjacent building at port

Canaveral. After the launch of the space shuttle is confirmed, commander Johnson will then inform the press corps that the mission new blue deal has commenced. After his announcement the press corps will be allowed to video and take pictures of the shuttle's departure. This was done as a security precaution. The president along with the other world leaders were notified that stage 1 of the new blue deal of restoring the Earth's ozone layer has been commenced. Foe the next three days the space shuttle will be traveling approximately 240,000 miles. That is the distance from the Earth to the Moon. Lieut Keaton was waiting for his turn for the next flight in the space shuttle known as Hope, but first he would have to wait on the report about the firmament counts of the lunar surface. Lieutenant Keaton was kept confined during those three days. Fearing the possibility of viruses or any other instances, he spent most of the time in confinement watching the progress of Captain Rylee and Lieutenant Downs. He also talked to Hannah back in El Paso. He assured her that he was all right and that everything was still on schedule. He told her to tell his mom he would be home shortly, but not to wait for him and not to leave supper in the microwave because he would be 240,000 miles away. Three days of isolation and Keaton had not heard a word. He was thinking to himself, "I hope nothing has gone wrong." On the fourth day of isolation, Lieutenant Keaton got a phone call from Captain Rylee saying, "It is from the Peak of Eternal Lights." Keaton said in a loud voice, "He's on the moon! Captain Rylee is calling me from the south pole of the moon."

Soon after getting the notice of Captain Rylee's call from the lunar surface, Lieutenant Keaton was released from the confinement Center and taken immediately to the Kennedy Space control center. Captain Rylee was then informed that Lieutenant Keaton was now present at the control center. Captain Rylee was being monitored from the lunar surface upon receiving the information. Captain Rylee said, "We have made it and it is beautiful here. The Peak of Eternal Lights is amazing." Keaton interrupted and said, "What about the Numerator?" They replied, "We've already started gathering the firmaments. The Numerator was a great success registering over 97%. Put on our space suit, we are awaiting your arrival." Keaton jokingly said, "I will be there as fast as I can travel 240,000 miles." Keaton left the control center and headed straight to the pre-flight coordination Center. Col Shea had heard the conversation between Captain Rylee and Keaton, but he had bad news for Keaton. When they came together Col Shea reluctantly told Keaton the launch of the space shuttle Hope had been postponed. Keaton said, "Postponed? Why sir?" Col Shea said, "The clouds are too dense. You don't want to have to put on all of the flight gear and have the flight aborted." Keaton explained, "I understand sir, but what are the prospects of the clouds lifting?" Col Shea said, "Not good. There is low visibility for the next 48 hours." Keaton said, "We don't have 48 hours to wait on the weather. The rest of the crew is on the moon and waiting on me." Col Shea told Keaton to keep his pants on so that they would launch him in the shuttle as soon as possible or when the weather was more clear. After a couple of hours, the clouds started to break up. "Someone must have been praying." Col Shea said. The launch was back on schedule and Keaton once again headed to the pre-flight coordination Center. It was from this location that he would be taken and assisted with putting on his space suit. He would be transported to the Space Shuttle that was waiting and fueled at the launching pad.

When Lieutenant Keaton arrived at the pre-flight center, Lieut Colby and Lieut Trenton was there to greet him. Keaton said, "What are you two doing here?" Lieut Trenton said, "We are going with you." Keaton asked, "You are going to the moon with me?" Lieut Colby said, "You didn't think you were going to have all the fun did you?" Col Shea walked into the building and said, "Keaton, keep your pants on. It was decided by me and the staff that the flight from Earth to the moon and back is quite a distance. You might need some company. We asked if there were any volunteers and these two knuckleheads came forward and said they would travel with you. Upon arrival, they will assist Lieut Massey with attaching and detaching the firmament canisters. I hope none of you have questions. Gentlemen, have a safe and profitable flight. I will see you back on Earth when the mission is completed."

Lieut Keaton and his other two companions were transported to the launchpad. When they arrived, they were assisted into the space shuttle Hope. While sitting in the space shuttle, they listened to the countdown. Finally, it reached T- 10 minutes and they could not keep their eyes off of the clock. They felt the rocket thrusters engage when the clock reached zero. They heard the announcement on the radio saying, "We have lifted off and the flight of the space shuttle is now on its way to the moon." For the next three days the astronauts spent time reminiscing about what got them there and what they were trained to do when they reached the Moon. Keaton spent some time thinking about Hannah. He told himself when he got back from the mission he was going to marry her. He said, "We are already engaged, so I gave her a ring. We have not set a date yet." He also thought of his father Jack. He kept thinking to himself that his dad was right because he became an astronaut. Keaton hoped he made his dad proud. He thought about his dad before the accident when he was five or six years old when he told Keaton he would become an astronaut and save the world.

Lieutenants Keaton, Colby, and Trenton's flight to the moon was just about over. It was all automated. Soon the space shuttle Hope was in orbit around the moon and all three men were staring out the windows trying to see the space station below. A voice from the radio said, "Welcome to the moon, prepare for landing procedures." They could hear the sound of the hydraulics from the lowering of the landing gear. Soon they would be on the lunar surface and the first leg of Keaton's mission would be completed. Everyone inside the lunar space station was filled with excitement and enthusiasm. Everyone would stay on the moon's surface for one night before the repair of the Earth's ozone layer would begin. Lieut Keaton could not sleep again that night, after hearing a live report from Captain Rylee about how the Numerator worked perfectly. Keaton felt somehow even though his dad had been gone for over 12 years, he was still overseeing this operation through some kind of divine power. When he began to try to close his eyes to get some sleep, he saw the Numerator sitting on the table inside the space station. Keaton went to sleep that night with full assurance that the mission was going to be a success.

The next morning the space station was moving with excitement. During the night, the space shuttle had been fitted and attached with the space rover Clean Sweep and a full canister of the moon's firmaments. Keaton had a good night's rest and a belly full of breakfast. He also had some homemade strawberry jam that was sent to him from Hannah. Col Shea allowed Lieut Trenton to smuggle it on board the shuttle. The commander of the moon station, The Peak of Eternal Light General Howard Mize walked into the dining facility. The order of attention was given and general Mize said, "This is a historic day. Lieut Keaton, it is a great honor of mine to present to you this day by the order of the secretary of the Space Force Academy that you shall be awarded the rank of Captain. Your first assignment as Captain is to order Lieut Colby and Lieut Trenton into the space shuttle. You are to accompany them to the international space competing for the second leg of the New Blue Deal restoring the ozone layer. After pinning the double bars on Captain Keaton along with his two companions, they headed for the space shuttle. The launch of the Space Shuttle along with the attached equipment should prove to be no problem. The moon's gravitational pull is much less than that of the Earth. Soon the space shuttle was on its second leg of the mission. Captain Keaton will arrive at the International Space Station and both Lieutenant Colby and Lieutenant Trenton will remain at the space station while captain Keaton flies through the stratosphere hopefully repairing the ozone layer. Lieutenant Trenton and Lieutenant Colby will assist Lieutenant Massey and her staff by switching the empty canisters from off the Space Shuttle and replacing it with a full canister when Captain

Keaton returns. This will be repeated until all five canisters are empty. Hopefully when this is finished and the mission is completed, the Earth's ozone layer will be restored. Three days later the space shuttle arrived at the International Space Station. While looking out through the windows, Captain Keaton saw four awaiting canisters. Just as soon as his companions had disembarked the space shuttle, Captain Keaton was ready to proceed to the ozone layer. It was then he was reminded that the space shuttle had to be refueled for the third leg of the mission. Keaton was so excited he could feel his heart beating inside his space suit. Within minutes from now, the fourth and final stage of the mission will commence. He had left the International Space Station and headed straight into the stratosphere when a voice came across the radio saying, "This is the president of the United States. All eyes in America and around the globe are watching you with hopefully optimism. We are told that when the moon's firmaments are released, we may be able to see a change in the sky with the natural eye. Until then, all of our prayers and wishes are with you Captain Keaton." Then, the radio went silent and the spaceship was gone from all radar screens. The command center at Kennedy Space Center was in shock. Then they heard Captain Keaton's voice come over the radio saying, "I am sorry. I think I may have accidentally hit the wrong button." Then they saw the sky begin to turn a dark blue. The space shuttle appeared as a speck in the sky, but behind the space shuttle where the firmaments had been released was a deep ocean blue color. Soon the canister was empty and Keaton returned to the international space station and replaced the canister. This was repeated until all five canisters were emptied.

Captain Keaton made three complete orbits around the Earth releasing the five canisters of the moon's firmaments.

Keaton started to hear the chatter from the International Space Station about how blue the Earth looked. People from across the globe were gazing into the sky in astonishment. All the oceans, rivers, and lakes seemed to be affected by this event. Tree scientists known as dendrology were reporting that trees are seemingly clapping their limbs together in jubilation of the repair of the ozone layer. A news outlet in Jerusalem reported that Eden had been restored. The word went out that Keaton found Eden. Jack and Keaton saved the world. Did Keaton and Hannah get married?

Printed in the United States
by Baker & Taylor Publisher Services